Part One

Chapter One

Ooh, someone must have been doing some decorating around here, Raven Baxter thought as she walked out of her English classroom and into the hallway at Bayside High School. Because that locker is looking *good*. She stopped in her tracks, a grin curling at the corners of her mouth. She particularly liked the way they'd added a tall, dark, and gorgeous guy standing right in front of it.

While his back was still turned toward her, Raven hurried over to the guy and placed her hands over his eyes. "Guess who?" she cooed. "She's sweet, adorable . . ." Raven cocked an eyebrow. ". . . and she's gonna get real mad if you get it wrong."

"Hey, Rae," Devon said, turning to face her.

Give that boy two points for correct guessing under pressure, Raven thought as she pulled away her hands. Of course, given that I call him after every class period, it's probably not too challenging to recognize my voice.

"Hey, you win a kiss . . ." Raven said brightly. She puckered up and leaned in for a little smooch. Mmmm, she thought as her heart fluttered in her chest. *De*licious. "Thank you very much." She smiled and pressed her hands together eagerly. "So, you wanna hang out tonight?"

Devon thought for a moment. "Um," he hedged, "tonight's not really good." He turned back to face his locker, and Raven was left looking at his black backpack.

For a minute, Raven wasn't sure what to say. Tonight's not good? she thought. I think he must mean, it's not good if we're *not* hanging out, right? Should I ask him to clarify?

Turning back to face Raven, Devon gave her an apologetic smile.

Okay, he means tonight's not good, period, she realized. But I'm not going to freak out and get all clingy girlfriend on him. Guys need space. Raven had read that in a magazine. Hunter time, it was called. Time to stare into the fire and think about . . . beasts. Or something. Anyway, guys needed it, and if Devon needed some hunter time, he was going to get it. "Okay," Raven said brightly, "I'm not gonna pry. You know, I'm not gonna be one of those girlfriends who's all up in your business."

Devon's face relaxed into a grin. "Oh, cool," he said warmly, his dark eyes glowing. "Thanks, Rae." He patted her on the shoulder and started to walk away.

"Bye!" Raven called sweetly as she watched his red shirt retreat down the hall. "Bye, Devon!

Bye, sweetie. I'll talk to you later, okay?"

Devon gave her a little wave.

"Somethin' is definitely going on with that boy," Raven announced, as her best friends, Chelsea Daniels and Eddie Thomas, walked over to join her. Raven narrowed her eyes. And I do not like it when something is going on with Devon . . . besides me, she thought.

Chelsea lifted her eyebrows. "You and Devon okay?"

"Oh, yeah, I'm fine." Raven cast a suspicious glance down the hallway, where Devon's back had just disappeared behind some double doors. "It's just he's been acting weird all week." She turned to her best guy friend. "Eddie, you're a guy, what do you think's going on?"

Eddie heaved a thoughtful sigh as he fidgeted with the strap on his black messenger bag. "Well, normally, Rae, when a guy acts like that, it means he's got something big on his mind," he said. "Or something small." He shrugged. "Or maybe he's just hungry."

Why do I ever ask Eddie's advice on relationships? Raven wondered as she gave her best guy friend a heavy-lidded glare. The boy is no Dr. Phil. "Why do you answer when you really don't even know?"

Eddie shook his head and grinned. "I'm a guy. It's what we do." With a little wave, he strutted off down the hall. "Holla."

Through her eye
The vision runs
Flash of future
Here it comes—

What's this? Devon and Chelsea, all cozy together by the lockers? Since when do those two tell each other secrets?

"Check this out."

Oooh, is Devon holding out what I think he's holding out? Okay, that's a little black velvet box. And there's only one thing that comes in a little black velvet box. . . .

Okay, I've known my girl Chelsea for a long time—but I've never seen her eyes bug out like that. Better tell her that it's not a good look.

"Oh, my goodness! Devon, this is beautiful. Raven's gonna love it!"

Oh, snap! A gift—for me?

And don't I always say that the best gifts come in teeny-tiny black boxes?

In the next moment, Raven was back in the present, looking into Chelsea's face. Raven put her hands over her eyes. "Chels!" she screeched. "I know why Devon has been acting weird. He bought me jewelry!" Her hands fluttered in front of her face, flapping in excitement.

"What?" Chelsea gave her a quit-playing look.

Oh, there she goes with that eyes-bugging-out thing, Raven thought. But she didn't have time to warn her friend—she was too excited about Devon!

Raven tossed her long, jet-black hair. "And Chelsea," she said breathlessly, "you're the one who saw it and you said—"

Chelsea's hand went to her chest. "What?"

" 'Oh, my goodness,' " Raven finished, " 'Raven's gonna love it.' "

"I did?" Chelsea shook her head and smiled proudly. "Raven, I love when I'm in your visions. It's like, it's like I'm starring in my own little movie that only you can see."

"That's adorable," Raven said sweetly. Then her tone turned serious. "Now listen up." She grabbed Chelsea's arm and pulled her in for a conference. "I want you to follow Devon, okay? Because you're the only one who knows what he got me." She squeezed her best friend's hand. I'm counting on you, Chelsea, she thought.

Chelsea seemed to get it. She nodded, her face serious. "Okay."

Time to put on some pressure. Raven wrapped her arm around Chelsea's shoulders. "As the star of my vision, I'm trusting you to make this one come true," Raven went on, gesturing grandly.

Chelsea bit her lip. "Right. Okay." She didn't move.

And why is the star of my vision still standing here in front of me? Raven wondered. "Well, what are you waiting for? Go on into the future with yourself!"

Chelsea rolled her eyes. "Well, Rae," she said in her hel-lo-what-do-you-*think*-I'm-waiting-for? voice, "you didn't say 'action.'"

Oh, there's going to be some action if this girl doesn't get going, Raven thought. But she was not about to upset the star of her most exciting vision ever. Without Chelsea, the vision wouldn't come true. And Raven wouldn't let that happen.

Chelsea pinned Devon in her sights—he was standing right by his locker. She'd tried to get him after every single class, but hadn't had any luck . . . yet. But he wasn't going to get away this time. Chelsea was as excited about starring in Raven's vision as Raven was about having it!

She slinked over to Devon and fluttered her eyelashes. "Oh, well, hello, Devon," Chelsea said brightly, gesturing to the empty hallway. She flipped her long, auburn hair and hitched her yellow backpack higher onto her shoulders. "Here we are, alone in the hallway. Just you and me and maybe, I don't know . . ." She poked Devon's arm and pressed her lips together. ". . . something sparkly?"

Devon blinked at her, confusion stamped across his face. "Why are you talking like that?"

"Why," Chelsea asked in her superperky voice, "whatever do you mean, you funny, funny boy?" She poked him playfully on the shoulder.

Devon sighed. "Look, Chels," he said patiently, as he opened his locker. "I'm going through kind of a weird time right now."

"Well, you should let it out," she said earnestly, desperate to make the vision come true for her best friend. "You know, it's not good to keep things in your heart, or your mind . . ." She touched Devon's head, then placed her hand on his shoulder. ". . . or your pocket." She smiled.

Devon thought for a moment. "Okay," he said finally. "Look, there's something I have to tell Raven, and I've been puttin' it off and puttin' it off, and I feel like I need to talk to someone. . . ."

"Ooh!" Chelsea raised her hand to volunteer. "You should talk to me."

"Okay." Nodding, Devon reached into the pocket of his baggy jeans. "Check this out." Holding out the small black velvet box, he snapped open the lid.

Chelsea gasped, putting her hand to her throat. "Oh, my goodness! Devon, that is beautiful. Raven's gonna love it!" She turned away slightly and lowered her voice. "Okay, Rae," she said. "I'm in the vision now."

Suddenly, Chelsea realized something. Something important. She turned back to face Devon. "That is a wedding ring," she said slowly, pointing to the little black velvet box. "Are you gonna ask Raven to marry you?"

"No." Devon's voice was thoughtful. "It's not for her." He looked down at the ground and—in one swift move—handed the box to Chelsea and dropped down onto one knee.

"Wh-whoa, Devon," Chelsea stuttered. "This is so sudden. I mean wow, I mean sure you know, you're an attractive guy, and I . . . but c'mon you're so young y'know, and Raven's my best friend. . . ."

Standing up, Devon gave Chelsea a look. "I guess I picked a bad time to tie my shoe," he said, taking the box from Chelsea's hand.

"Ya think?" Chelsea shot back.

"Look, the ring's for my father," Devon explained. "I mean, he's getting remarried tonight and I'm his best man."

"Aww, how sweet." Chelsea smiled at the explanation. But when she thought about it for a moment, she realized that it didn't make sense. Devon's father getting married shouldn't be a secret from Raven. "Why didn't you tell Raven about this?"

"There's more to the story." He shook his head, wincing. "Oh, man . . ."

Chelsea felt her stomach lurch. Something about Devon's face told her that the "more" to the story was . . . well, not good. "What?" she asked. "What is it?"

"Look, Raven has to hear this from me, okay?" Devon put his hand against his chest, his dark eyes serious. "So you have to promise me you won't tell her."

Chelsea nodded. She knew that she didn't have a choice. She put up her hand in her very best scout's-honor pledge. "I promise."

Chapter Two

Mr. and Mrs. Baxter were in the kitchen, sipping coffee. It was their favorite way to unwind together in the afternoon before Raven's dad headed off to the restaurant. It was peaceful and quiet. . . .

"Mom, Dad!" Cory cried as he burst through the kitchen door.

Well, it was usually peaceful and quiet.

"Happy anniversary!" Cory held out an oversized orange shopping bag.

Mrs. Baxter smiled. "Cory, that's so thoughtful," she said as she got down from her tall stool. She gave Cory a kiss on the cheek. "But, honey, our anniversary isn't until next month."

"But we will take the present now," Mr. Baxter said as he snatched the gift from his wife and hurried over to the booth in the corner. "Thank you."

"I was gonna wait . . ." Cory shrugged. ". . . but I saw the perfect thing, and I just had to get it for you."

Mr. Baxter opened the bag and pulled out a large box.

"Honey, that's so sweet," Mrs. Baxter said as she studied the box. Her smile faltered as she read the script across the front. "Look," she said, forcing herself to sound excited, "it's . . . it's Clucky, the Singing Chicken."

Mrs. Baxter opened the box and pulled out a wooden plaque. A rubber chicken was glued to the front. As she stared at it, the chicken started to cluck a waltz. Mrs. Baxter glanced nervously at Cory's excited face. Nope, the gift wasn't a joke. Her son seriously thought this was the best present ever.

Mr. and Mrs. Baxter exchanged a look as Cory burst out laughing.

"How great is this?" Cory demanded, grinning madly at the chicken.

Mr. Baxter tried to chuckle along. "Well, uh, thank you very much, Cory," he said. "We are certainly gonna enjoy this one." He put Clucky back in the box and closed the lid. Clucky stopped clucking. Thank goodness.

Cory's face fell. "Wait—wait Dad. Aren't you gonna hang Clucky up?"

Mrs. Baxter glanced around her tastefully decorated kitchen. She had actually been thinking that Clucky would be a perfect addition to the back of the closet. He was the most annoying invention ever! "Where?" she asked, trying to hide the concern in her voice.

Cory gestured to the wall behind his father's head. "Right up there on the wall."

A blank wall. Mrs. Baxter couldn't believe she had let this happen.

"Uh, you know I would," Mr. Baxter hedged, "but I, uh . . . misplaced the hammer."

Mrs. Baxter nodded slightly. It was a lie—but sometimes lying was okay, when it meant you wouldn't have to listen to clucking every time you went into the kitchen for a snack.

"Don't worry about it," Cory said confidently. "I got the hook up."

"Cory," Mr. Baxter said, "I don't need any help buying a hammer."

"No, Dad." Cory pointed to the top of the blank space on the wall. "I got the hook up on the wall!"

Cory's parents stared up at the hook in horror.

"Oh," Mr. Baxter said slowly, "I guess . . . then . . . there's no reason not to hang up

Clucky. Unless . . . Tanya?" He looked hopefully at his wife.

She shook her head. "I got nothin'."

Mr. Baxter heaved a sigh. "Well, then . . ." Clearing his throat, Mr. Baxter hung Clucky on the wall. The rubber chicken clucked away.

Cory laughed. "The coolest part is his eyes have a motion detector," he explained. "So every time you walk by, he clucks, we laugh."

Cackling, Cory walked out of the kitchen. Mr. and Mrs. Baxter looked up at Clucky as he clucked his little rubber heart out. They tried to laugh at his irritating mechanical clucks.

Tried. And failed.

What is wrong with that girl? Raven wondered as she and Chelsea walked into the kitchen. She's had her nose buried in that bubble-gum comic for the past three blocks! Doesn't she know that information on Devon is on a need-to-know basis . . . and I need to know where my jewelry is—now!

Chelsea kept her eyes on the comic and giggled.

"Hey, Chels, you need to stop reading and tell me what's happening with Devon," Raven said, cocking an eyebrow at her best friend. She took off her backpack and dropped it onto the kitchen counter.

Chelsea shook her head and didn't put down the comic. "Rae, I'm sorry, but I love these comics!" she insisted. "Bubble Gum Jim is so funny!"

This is about to get seriously unfunny real fast! Raven thought. "Chels!" she cried, pounding her fist against the flat of her hand. "What is going on?"

"Oh, okay." Chelsea tried to hold back her

giggles. "I'm sorry, okay." She held out the comic. "The reason he threw the clock out the window is because he wanted to see time fly. Get it? It's so funny!"

"Hey, Chels," Raven said as she narrowed her eyes dangerously and planted a hand on her hip, "you're gonna see something fly if you don't stop changing the subject and tell me what Devon said."

Finally dropping the act, Chelsea heaved a sigh. "I'm sorry," she said honestly, "I can't. I promised him I wouldn't say anything." She reached into Raven's fridge for a drink.

Raven's jaw dropped. *Oh, I know I'm not hearing what I think I'm hearing.* "Are you . . . ?" She shook her head. "Chels, when we were six, we made a promise that we would tell each other everything. So, which promise is more important?" she demanded.

Looking pained, Chelsea thought about

it. "Well . . ." she admitted, "you are my best friend, y'know. And, y'know, I'm probably not gonna see Devon again."

Whoa, whoa, hold up. Not going to see Devon again? I hope that there was something in that bubble gum, because Chelsea is talking crazy. Raven's mouth went dry.

"And he didn't want to marry me, anyway," Chelsea went on, half to herself. Just then, she caught sight of the new addition to the Baxters' kitchen. "What?" she cried, pointing to the rubber chicken on the wall. "Is that Clucky, the Singing Chicken? What?" She hurried over to Clucky and waved in front of his beak. The robotic clucking began.

Chelsea cracked up as the waltz clucked on. "Ah," she said with a happy sigh, "endlessly hilarious. So funny."

Raven looked up at the chicken. Wow, if she thinks that's funny, then there really was something in that gum, Raven thought. Why did Mom ever let that thing in here in the first place? "Okay, Chels," she said as patiently as she could, "I need you to rewind to the marrying part, are you with me?" She yanked her best friend out of Clucky's line of sight. "Okay, and tell me how that came up?"

"Well," Chelsea said, studying the linoleum, "I guess it all came up with the wedding ring."

Raven gasped. "There was a wedding ring?" she asked, giggling. A chill ran through her body, from her head to her toes. Devon does love me! she thought. Those daisy petals I plucked last Thursday were right! You go, psychic flower!

"Yeah," Chelsea said, "it was just like in your vision, Rae. But before you get excited, it wasn't for you." She paused for a moment, remembering Devon dropping to one knee. "Or for me. It was for Chandra."

"Oh, Chandra," Raven said, nodding. Of course . . . Wait a minute—that makes no sense! "Who the heck is Chandra?"

"Look, maybe I should just start from the beginning," Chelsea suggested.

Raven nodded. "Yeah, that would be nice." She folded her arms across her chest.

"Devon's dad is getting remarried to a woman named Chandra," Chelsea explained, "and, um, Devon is the best man, so that's why he was carrying the ring."

"Oh, okay." Raven nodded. The explanation made sense, but Raven couldn't help feeling a little disappointed. Besides, there was something that Chelsea had left out. "So, um, Chels, let's get to the part about never seeing Devon again."

"Um, Rae." Chelsea pressed her lips together. "That's the hard part. He doesn't really know how to tell you." She winced.

"You tell me," Raven begged gently. If it's bad news, I'd rather hear it from my best friend than anyone else, she thought. And something told her it was bad news.

"Okay, Rae," Chelsea said finally. "Um, Chandra lives in Seattle, and Devon and his whole family are going to move there."

Raven's head swam. Fighting the dizziness, she sat down on a kitchen stool. "Seattle?" she repeated.

"Yeah, Rae," Chelsea said encouragingly, "it's not that far."

Sure—not as far as New York. Or Tokyo. Or South Africa. But it's not even in this state. It's not like I have a private jet and can just go over to Devon's house whenever I want to say hey. It's not like we can have lunch together. Or go to a movie. Or even hug. "Chels," Raven said, fighting tears, "it might as well be on the other side of the world."

Chelsea reached for her friend and pulled her into a hug. "I'm sorry, Rae."

Raven swallowed hard. She felt a hot tear escape and trickle down the side of her nose. So am I, she thought miserably. So am I.

Chapter Three

Raven lay on her bed, staring up at the ceiling. *This can't be happening,* she thought miserably. *My boyfriend can't be moving away from San Francisco. It's too cruel and unusual!* Sighing, she pulled a chocolate chip cookie from the bag lying on her stomach and munched it.

Chelsea sat cross-legged on the floor near Raven's feet.

Gotta give my girl credit, Raven thought. *She hasn't moved from my side since she told me the bad news. And besides, she knows what a broken heart needs.* Raven reached into the bag of cookies again.

"Hey, Rae," Eddie said as he flung open

the door to Raven's room. "I got here as soon I could. I can't believe Devon is movin' away."

Raven blinked at him. "What's the point of being psychic if I couldn't see this coming?" she wailed.

"Oh, that's messed up," Eddie agreed as he settled onto the foot of Raven's bed. "He really should've told you, Rae."

"Well, he wanted to," Chelsea said, remembering how miserable Devon had looked when he told her that he was moving away. "He just didn't really know how."

"How about just stepping up and saying it?" Eddie snapped.

"Oh, c'mon," Chelsea countered, "he didn't want to break her heart."

"And this is better, Chels?" Eddie shot back. He gestured toward Raven, who had stuck her face halfway into the bag of treats.

"A broken woman looking for happiness at the bottom of an empty cookie bag?"

Raven, whose face was covered in crumbs and chocolate goo, agreed. "You're right," she said, brushing the crumbs from her face, "this is pathetic. I'm gonna take some action." She thought for a moment—and then her face brightened. "I'm gonna get more cookies!" she said as she crawled toward the end of the bed.

Eddie stepped in her way. "Rae . . ."

"Okay, you're right," Raven said, flopping back against her pillows. She reached for the cordless and started punching in a number. "I'm gonna call Devon." She smiled wickedly. "And then I'm gonna get more cookies."

"No, give me the phone." Chelsea grabbed it out of Raven's hand before she could press TALK. "You're not gonna call Devon! Then he's gonna know I broke my promise and that I told you."

"Well, what am I gonna do, sit here and do nothing?" Raven cried. I mean, come on, she thought. That doesn't sound like me, does it?

"Rae, it doesn't even matter if you talk to Devon, okay?" Chelsea pointed out. "His father's the one getting married."

"Well, then, maybe I need to talk to his father," Raven suggested.

Eddie rolled his eyes. "And say what? 'I love your son, please don't move'?"

Raven nodded. "Yeah. Why not? What do I have to lose? If he sees how much we care about each other, maybe he'll change his mind about moving."

"Okay," Chelsea said. "Well, Rae, you better talk to him pretty soon."

"Well, why?" Raven asked.

Chelsea lifted her eyebrows. "Because they're moving right after the wedding."

Raven shrugged. "Okay. When's the wedding?"

Chelsea checked her watch. "Uh, well . . . looks like right now."

"Oh, snap!" Raven shouted, lunging off the bed and out the door. I've gotta get there right away! I've gotta talk to Devon's dad and make him see reason! Nothing's gonna stop me! Nothing!

Eddie and Chelsea looked at each other as Raven's footsteps thundered down the hall . . . and then thundered back. She poked her head back into her room.

"Anybody know where the wedding is?" Raven asked.

Ooh, this is like my dream wedding, Raven thought as she peeked out from behind a multicolored flower arrangement. Gentle organ music floated through the air. The minister was at his place at the altar as well-dressed guests filed in and took their seats amid flower-bedecked pews.

The only thing wrong is that this isn't *my* wedding, Raven added mentally. And it isn't a dream.

"Okay!" Raven whispered to her friends. "The ceremony is starting."

Raven froze as Devon—looking hot enough to melt steel—gave his father a hug and started down the aisle.

Raven clenched her teeth. "Devon is lookin' fine in that tuxedo." She leaned out from behind the pillar of flowers to get a better look.

Chelsea yanked her back. "Okay, Rae," she said, snapping her fingers in front of Raven's face. "Hey, hey, focus."

Raven took a deep breath. "Right," she said to herself. "Right, right, okay."

Devon stepped up to the altar and nodded at the minister as his father looked on anxiously. The organist paused.

"Hey, hey," Eddie said, giving Raven a nudge. "His dad hasn't gone down the aisle yet. You still have a chance. Just don't let Devon see you. Y'know what I'm sayin'?"

"Right." Raven squared her shoulders. "C'mon."

"All right." Eddie nodded at her encouragingly. "Do that."

But how am I going to sneak up to Mr. Carter without Devon seeing me? Raven wondered, looking around for inspiration. Suddenly, she found it—in a vase. Raven grabbed a bunch of flowers and held them in front of her face.

"Mr. Carter," Raven whispered.

Devon's dad was still peering nervously down the aisle. He didn't hear her.

"Mr. Carter," Raven repeated, louder this time.

Okay, it's starting to look like Devon's dad needs to get his hearing checked, Raven thought. She pulled down the flowers. "Carter!" she shouted.

Raven pulled the flowers back up to her face as Devon's dad jumped, then whipped around.

"Right," Raven said brightly. Okay, that worked. Now—what do I say? She thought fast. "Great. You probably don't know it, but you probably heard of me. I'm Raven."

Mr. Carter looked confused . . . and concerned. Like maybe this talking bunch of flowers was a little . . . crazy.

"Um, I really don't want Devon to see me," Raven explained. "It's complicated, but some promises were made. . . ."

Suddenly, the organ music began again. Mr. Carter straightened his tuxedo jacket. "Now it's really nice chatting with you," Mr. Carter said, turning to look back down the aisle, "but I kinda made some promises of my own." He started to walk down the aisle, but Raven wasn't about to let him get away that easily.

"No, but I really need to talk to you," she whispered as she tagged after him, squatting to hide from Devon. Oh, please, just let me look like a walking bouquet, she begged silently. "It's only gonna take a second."

"Well, you better talk fast," Mr. Carter said. He was already walking away.

Raven started after him when, suddenly, a large . . . object . . . got in her way, tripping her.

"Oof!" Raven sprawled to the floor as Mr. Carter headed toward the altar.

He's getting away! Raven thought wildly. Who tripped me? Who would be so cruel? So inhumane? So—

"Hello, Raven," Nadine said, smiling down

at Raven with an evil twinkle in her eye. "We meet again."

Ooh, she's the evilest little flower girl ever! Raven thought. Why is she wearing a little white dress and carrying a basket when she needs horns and a pitchfork instead?

"Hey," Raven said as cheerfully as she could, "it's Devon's adorable little sister. How ya been, Deenie?"

Nadine narrowed her eyes to dangerous little slits. "I'm glad you're here. Now we can say good-bye." She smiled smugly. "Forever."

Nadine tossed a handful of rose petals in Raven's face. One of them got caught in her lip gloss.

Pretty good arm for a six-year-old, Raven thought as she spat out a mouthful of petals.

Nadine pranced off, tossing flower petals from her basket as Raven hurried back down the aisle to rejoin her friends.

"Hey, you work things out with Mr. Carter?" Chelsea asked hopefully.

"No." She held her thumb and forefinger centimeters apart. "I was this close. I just needed another second." She glanced over her shoulder just as Devon looked out at the gathered guests.

"Oh, snap!" Raven cried, hitting the deck. Her friends followed her behind a pew. "Duck! I don't want Devon to see us." She peered out. The coast was clear. "Okay, Eddie, listen. I want you to stay here and stall. Chelsea, you come with me. We're gonna figure out our next move."

Chelsea nodded. "All right. Snap. Duck. Stall. Move. Got it."

Raven and Chelsea scurried back into the foyer as Eddie rolled across the aisle and G.I. Joe'd toward the organist. Then he stood up, brushed himself off, and tapped the organ player on the shoulder. The elegantly dressed gentleman looked up at Eddie.

"I'm from the organ players' union," Eddie explained. "It's time for your break."

With a shrug, the organist got up and walked off. Eddie took his seat. He was going to stall for all he was worth. He started playing one of the few organ tunes he knew.

"Charge!" cried someone from the crowd as Eddie finished his song. Eddie pumped his fist. Looked like at least one of these people had been to a baseball game.

Chapter Four

What's this? Raven thought as she grabbed the doorknob and flung open the door. Who cares? We just need to hide! She and Chelsea ducked into the small room and shut the door.

"Okay, Chels," Raven said, pacing. "We have to figure out a way to get to Mr. Carter. Now think."

"Okay." Chelsea squeezed her eyes shut and grimaced, letting out small grunting noises.

Man, I didn't realize I was giving Chels such a tough assignment, Raven thought as she eyed her friend. "Don't hurt yourself."

"Momma," called a woman's voice, "is that you?"

That was when Raven realized that there was another door inside the room. Like it might lead to a bathroom. Oh, nuh-unh, Raven thought as she looked around. Fluffy veil . . . billowy white dress . . . we're in the bride's dressing room!

"It's the bride!" Raven hissed. And she just heard us!

"Omigosh!" Chelsea nudged her best friend. "Say something, say something!"

Why do I always have to say something? But there was no time to argue. Okay, Raven, think—how would Chandra's mother sound? She deepened her voice. "Yes, baby," Raven improvised. "It's me, I'm your momma." She grimaced at her best friend, who motioned for her to keep going. "How ya doin', child?"

"I'm gonna be a while," Chandra admitted through the bathroom door.

Raven clapped silently. What luck!

"It's my stomach," Chandra went on. "I shouldn't have had all those chili dogs at my bachelorette party."

Oh, ew. "Nasty," Raven whispered. That is way more than I wanted to know about Devon's future stepmother.

Chelsea looked ill.

Okay, just keep going, Raven told herself. "Okay, baby," she said in her deep "momma" voice, "well, just take your time, and your man is not going anywhere. Not going anywhere. He's just gonna . . ." Suddenly, the billowy white dress caught Raven's eye. ". . . stay right here." Toying with a sleeve, she looked up at her friend. "Chels?"

Chelsea looked horrified. "You wouldn't."

Raven nodded. "Then I shouldn't." But what other way is there to get to Mr. Carter?

Chelsea must have had the same thought. "But you must."

A gleam came into Raven's eye. "Then I will."

"Are you sure?"

Raven hesitated. "I don't know."

Chelsea studied the dress. "Yeah."

I mean, it would never work, Raven told herself. There's no way . . . unless . . .

"Wait," Mrs. Baxter said as she stopped her husband from walking into the kitchen, "don't let Clucky see us."

"Oh, right." Mr. Baxter nodded, realizing that his wife had just stopped him from making a terrible mistake. Once Clucky got started, he didn't stop. "Wait, why are we whispering? Clucky has a motion detector."

"He might see our lips moving," Mrs. Baxter explained.

They looked over at Clucky's beady little eyes. They were always watching. Always . . . watching . . .

Raven's parents exchanged a look, then dropped to the floor.

"Stay low," Mrs. Baxter commanded as she slithered toward the refrigerator. Mr. Baxter slid against the wall, then reached for two glasses from the shelf.

With a quick move, Mrs. Baxter removed the grapefruit juice from the bottom shelf of the fridge then slunk, snakelike, toward her husband.

Mr. Baxter eyed the juice. "You forgot ice."

Mrs. Baxter glanced over her shoulder at the fridge. "I can't go back, it's too dangerous."

"That's it," Mr. Baxter announced. "I can't take it anymore! We can't even walk around our own house without hearing that stupid clucking chicken!" He stood up, and Clucky began his clucking waltz.

He moved toward the rubber chicken and grabbed it from the wall.

Mrs. Baxter grabbed his arm. "Well, don't break Clucky." She gave her husband a warning look. "Let me do it."

Mr. Baxter reached for the plaque. "No, no," he said, flipping it over. "Let me just take the batteries out. Ha-ha. You have run out of clucking," he taunted as he pulled the batteries from Clucky's rear panel.

At that moment, Cory walked into the kitchen. "Dad!" he cried, staring at the rubber chicken in his father's hands. "What are you doing?"

"Uh . . ." Mr. Baxter flashed his son a guilty look.

Cory noticed the batteries that his father was holding. "Oh, you don't have to change the batteries," he said brightly. "They're just for backup. He's got a built-in power system."

"Well . . ." Mrs. Baxter looked down at the annoying chicken who would, apparently, never stop clucking. Oh, the horror! "They think of everything."

"Don't worry, guys," Cory assured them. "Clucky's gonna cluck forever."

Mr. and Mrs. Baxter shared a look as their son walked out of the room.

That was exactly what they were afraid of.

Eddie was starting to get into this organ-playing thing. He hummed along as he played. If you're happy and you know it . . . he signaled the crowd.

Clap, clap!

The crowd was clearly confused, but they were playing along. Eddie respected them for that.

"You're not the organ player!"

Eddie looked up to see an angelic little girl in white glaring at him. "Of course I am, little girl," he said nervously. He pointed at the organ. "This is an organ, and I'm playing it."

Nadine narrowed her eyes. "Well, it's time to play 'Here Comes the Bride.'"

Eddie cocked his eyebrow. He wasn't about to let some pipsqueak little girl boss him around—not when Raven was counting on him. And when the crowd was so into the song. "And if I don't?" he challenged.

Nadine glared at Eddie, who was starting to realize that this little flower girl meant business.

A moment later, he was spitting out flower petals and playing the opening bars to "Here Comes the Bride."

Nadine stepped out sweetly, delicately scattering flower petals from her basket across the aisle.

And right on time, the bride appeared at the end of the aisle, her face hidden by a flowing veil.

Eddie didn't have time to feel bad about the fact that things didn't work out for Raven, because just then, the bride lifted her veil and gave him a look.

Eddie nearly fell off his organ bench. That was no bride! That was Raven!

Chelsea rushed over to Eddie. "Play faster!" she whispered. "Here's the deal, Raven kind of borrowed the bride's wedding gown, so if she doesn't get down that aisle in a hurry, things are gonna get pretty ugly."

"Oh, I hear ya," Eddie said, nodding. "Okay, let's do something." He didn't miss a beat. He just kept playing "Here Comes the Bride" . . . double-time.

Raven and Nadine quickened their step and were at the altar in seconds. Raven took her place beside Mr. Carter, and the minister stood before them. He was a serious-looking man with glasses and a long, brightly colored strip of African fabric running down the lapels of his black suit.

"Dearly beloved . . ." he began, "we are gathered here today to join this man and this woman . . ."

Okay, time to make something happen, Raven decided. Before I accidentally get married to Devon's dad! "We have to talk," she whispered in Mr. Carter's ear.

The minister flashed her a confused look.

"Honey," Mr. Carter said patiently, "we're about to be married." He smiled at the minister. "She's just a little bit nervous."

The minister cleared his throat. "Moving right along." He looked out at the guests. "If anyone present has any objections to this—"

Oh, snap! It's now or never! "Yeah, I do," Raven piped up, lifting her hand.

Mr. Carter patted her arm. "Honey, the 'I dos' don't come until later." He gestured toward the reverend, who looked extremely worried. "Please, continue with the ceremony."

"No, you can't," Raven insisted. She faced Mr. Carter. "I love your son."

A gasp went up from the crowd.

Devon looked like he was about to faint.

Okay . . . that didn't exactly come out right. "Oh, no," Raven said to the guests. "Y'all don't understand. I'm only fifteen."

This time, the gasp was so loud that Raven was surprised the guests didn't manage to inhale part of the altar.

"Ooh, no, no, no." This is getting out of control. It's time to take drastic measures. "I'm not the bride!" Raven flipped back the veil.

"Oh," the crowd chorused.

"Raven?" Devon's face held a mix of emotions—happiness to see her, confusion, concern.

And he still looks fine in that tuxedo, Raven decided.

"Raven," Nadine spat through gritted teeth. She moved toward Raven—no doubt to do more damage with her flower petals—but Devon stopped her.

"So where's my bride?" Mr. Carter demanded.

"Oh!" Right, I guess I should explain that . . . minus some of the details. "There was a party and some chili dogs . . ." Okay, already too much information. Raven decided to go back to the most important subject. "But Mr. Carter, I wanted to talk to you before you moved." She glanced over at her boyfriend. Her heart fluttered. Wow, I'm really crazy about that guy, she realized. "Devon and I have something really special, and if you move to Seattle it'll be over. So, I came here to ask you . . ." She had to swallow hard to keep from crying. "Please, please, don't go."

Mr. Carter looked like he couldn't believe

his ears. "Let me get this straight. You crashed my wedding, you stole the gown, you impersonated my bride, and then you just—"

Raven rolled her eyes. "You know what? If you lump it together like that, it's gonna sound bad, but if you separated it and got to the root of the situation . . ."

"Dad." Devon stepped forward. "Can I have a second with Raven, please?"

Mr. Carter threw up his hands. "Oh, yeah, just don't mind me, I'm just looking for my bride." He called out, "Chandra?"

"Rae," Devon said, taking her hand, "I know all of this is happening so fast, but I mean, look at my dad. He's never been happier."

Raven looked over at Mr. Carter.

Actually, he looks kind of traumatized right now, she thought. But I guess that's kind of my fault.

"Well," Devon went on quickly, "my point

is, we're moving, and he's not gonna change his mind."

Raven looked at the floor. "Yeah," she said quietly. "It was kinda crazy for me to come here, wasn't it?" She looked up into Devon's face. "I just had to give it a shot."

"Look, Rae, I'm sorry I didn't tell you about all of this." Devon looked around at the wedding. "I mean, I was gonna come over and talk before we left."

"You can talk now," Raven told him.

"Okay. Look, I think you're really amazing. And I'll never forget you."

Hot tears pooled in Raven's eyes. "Will I ever see you again?"

"I hope so," Devon said earnestly. "I love you, Rae."

"I love you, too, Devon."

Devon leaned forward and pressed his lips against Raven's.

What's that? Is that—applause? Looking up, Raven realized that the guests were clapping for her and her boyfriend.

Back by the organ, Chelsea teared up. "Weddings always kinda make me cry," she explained.

With a grin, Eddie launched into the recessional march.

Suddenly, an earsplitting whistle rang through the hall. "Hold it!" the minister shouted. "No one's gotten married yet."

Realizing that the minister actually had a good point, Eddie pulled his hands off the keyboard.

"Seriously," Mr. Carter said to the guests, "has anyone seen Chandra?"

Just then, a tall woman in a white satin bathrobe appeared at the end of the aisle.

Oh, she's pretty! Raven thought when she caught sight of the bride for the first time. Pretty angry!

Chandra pointed furiously at Raven. "She stole my dress and my husband!"

"Yeah," Raven said to Mr. Carter, "I think I spotted her."

Chandra stomped toward Raven.

Okay, think fast! Raven tossed the bouquet at the oncoming Bridezilla. "Catch!"

As though she had been waiting for this moment all of her life, Chandra caught the bouquet. She looked down at the flowers.

I guess it's time to give back the dress and the veil, Raven thought sadly. Too bad. I was kind of enjoying being a bride!

Chapter Five

"I now pronounce you husband and wife," the minister said as Raven, Chelsea, and Eddie watched from the back pew.

Mr. Carter leaned toward Chandra, who was looking gorgeous now that she was back in her wedding dress . . . and, you know, finished with the chili dogs.

The organist—back from his break—played the recessional as the bride and groom exchanged a kiss.

The guests burst into applause as the bride and groom headed down the aisle together. Devon followed. He glanced at Raven.

He looks like I feel, Raven thought. *And I feel . . . awful.*

Devon paused at her pew. "Good-bye, Rae."

Don't cry, don't cry, don't cry, Raven commanded herself. At least, not until he's gone. "Bye, Devon."

Sadly, Devon continued up the aisle. But once he reached his father, Nadine, and Chandra, Devon's family swept him into an enormous hug. They walked out of the hall together.

Chelsea and Eddie wrapped Raven into a group hug of their own.

The tears were threatening to take over, but Raven smiled anyway.

She might not have her boyfriend . . . but she'd always have her friends.

It was two weeks later, and Clucky was still clucking away.

Mr. and Mrs. Baxter didn't even hear him anymore. Because they wore earplugs whenever they were in the kitchen.

"Mom, Dad," Raven said seriously as she sat down at the kitchen counter.

They continued making dinner.

Raven tried again. "MOM!" she shouted. "DAD!" She gestured toward her ears. "Mom, ears."

Getting the message, Mr. and Mrs. Baxter removed their earplugs.

Raven sighed. "Listen," she said shakily, "I have tried to be strong these past couple of weeks. But I'm about to crack."

Mrs. Baxter put her hand on her daughter's shoulder. "Rae, honey," she said, "I thought you were starting to be okay with Devon moving."

"Oh, I am, Mom." Raven cast a dangerous glare at Clucky. "Mom, it's that chicken! Dang, why can't Clucky move to Seattle?"

Mrs. Baxter lifted her eyebrows. "Who you

tellin'?" She turned to her husband. "Look, y'know, Raven's right. We should just explain to Cory that his very appreciated and thoughtful gift is driving us up the wall."

Speak of the devil, Raven thought as Cory appeared at that very moment. He strode into the kitchen with an enormous shopping bag, and the look on his face said that he was dead serious about . . . something.

Before anyone could say a word, Cory ripped Clucky from the wall and shut off the mechanical clucking.

Cory heaved a sigh. "Phew, yes," he said under his breath. He looked up at the rest of his family. "I don't know about you guys, but Clucky was pluckin' my last nerve."

Mr. and Mrs. Baxter exchanged a relieved look.

Oh, good, Raven thought. Now I don't have to kill Clucky—or Cory.

"Yeah," Mr. Baxter admitted. "That act was getting kinda old."

"Aww, we're gonna miss him," Raven said sarcastically. "Clucky, buh-bye."

"And hello, Sir Quackington!" Cory added, pulling a large box from his shopping bag. He held up a wooden plaque—with a rubber duck head.

Mrs. Baxter gave the duck a nervous glance as Cory hung him up on the wall. "Does Sir Quackington sing?"

Cory shook his head. "No."

The rest of the Baxters let out a sigh of relief.

Cory grinned. "He makes wise . . . quacks!" He cracked up.

"You're ugly! Quack, quack," Sir Quackington said. "Your breath stinks. Quack, quack. You got a big head. Quack! Quack! Quack! Quack!"

Cory cackled. "Sir Quackington quacks me up!"

Ooh, something's gonna quack! Raven thought. And it isn't just a rubber duck!

"Look, Raven has to hear this from me, okay?"
Devon said to Chelsea. "So you have to
promise me you won't tell her."

"Mom! Dad!" Cory cried. "Happy anniversary!"

Mr. Baxter reluctantly hung Clucky the Singing Chicken—the Baxters' anniversary gift from Cory.

"Hey, Chels, you need to stop reading and tell me what's happening with Devon," Raven said.

"Honey," Mrs. Baxter said in a patient voice, "you cannot accept this dress. It's way too extravagant."

Raven unrolled the scroll and announced, "It's an invitation. He's throwing a party at the embassy!"

"Since you put on the dress and came down here, you accepted," Eddie told Raven.

"I'm sorry I ruined our wedding. I hope you'll forgive me. Can we still be friends?" Raven asked hopefully.

that's **SO** raven

Part Two

Chapter One

Raven nearly floated down the stairs in the hallway at school, turning heads as she went. She was wearing a denim shirt and a matching pair of jeans, both with silver embroidery. Her hair was done in an elaborate do—two ponytails at the top of her head, from which her superlong hair cascaded to her shoulders in tiny braids. Hello, world! Raven thought, grinning. Are you ready for my fashion statement? Because here it is: Raven is looking good.

Just then, Chelsea caught sight of the outfit. "Whoa, Rae," Chelsea said, nodding in admiration as Raven took a spin, giving her the full effect. "Seriously, whoa."

Raven smiled. "I did outdo myself if I do

say so . . ." She planted her hands on her hips. ". . . myself."

"Y'know everybody gonna be talkin' about this little getup right here." Eddie pointed at the silver braid that twined up the side of Raven's leg.

Raven batted her eyelashes. "Well, if they have to talk," she said innocently, "they might as well talk about *moi*."

"Or *him*," Chelsea added, pointing.

What? Raven peered down the hall. Is someone trying to steal my fashion spotlight?

A cute guy who Raven had never seen before was headed toward the lockers. He was wearing a tunic and baggy pants made from wild African fabric. He had on a matching hat and wore a bag slung across his chest. The boy is kickin' it tribal style, Raven thought approvingly. It's bold.

Suddenly, she realized that Chelsea wasn't

the only person pointing at the cute boy. Chelsea was right—people were talking.

"They're not talking about him," Eddie corrected. "They're laughing at him."

Raven frowned. Sure enough, the fashion police of Bayside High had gathered in a circle. The cute boy cringed as the students snickered at his outfit. He touched his hat self-consciously.

"That's not nice," Raven said, stomping over to the little group that had descended, locust-style, around the cute boy. "Excuse me, people!" Raven snapped her fingers at the crowd. "Hey! How y'all doin'? I know you all are not having a fashion problem in this area." She pointed at the style-impaired group. "'Cause y'all should not be talkin'." She picked out the students one by one and critiqued their taste. "You last-season-shoe wearin', twelve-year-old-shirt-sportin', vest-with-anundershirt . . . And you." She glared at a girl in a wide-shouldered blue shirt. "I will call you when shoulder pads come back, okay? Which is . . . never!" Raven waved as the students skulked off. "Good-bye!" She straightened her shirt and started to walk away.

The cute boy followed her. "Thank you," he said with a smile. His speech was lightly accented, and he chose his words carefully. "That was very brave. Not unlike a mother lion protecting her young from a pack of hyenas."

Hyenas, Raven thought. The boy certainly understands this place. And he has a gift for the weird metaphor. "Okay, no problem," Raven told him. "No problem. Ummm." She gestured at his outfit. "You look good, all right? No worries."

"Thank you," the boy said. "So do you."

See? I knew this boy had an eye for good

fashion! He understood my statement! "Thank you," Raven said warmly. "I'm Raven."

The boy placed his palm over his chest. "I am Tendaji. An exchange student from the country of Shakobi."

"Shakobi!" Raven had heard of it—it was somewhere in Africa. She suddenly had a new appreciation for Tendaji's outfit. "Wow, well, nice to meet you, Tendaji." She motioned toward her peeps. "These are my best friends, Eddie and Chelsea."

"What's up?" Eddie laughed, like he couldn't believe he was actually meeting someone from Africa right by the lockers. He slapped Tendaji's hand.

"Welcome to America," Chelsea said seriously, as though she was part of a presidential delegation.

"You can chill with us after school," Raven told Tendaji.

"Chill?" Tendaji repeated, looking concerned. "Are you expecting a drop in temperature?"

Raven smiled. Whoops! Guess something didn't translate. "No, no, no," she explained. "Enjoy each other's company."

Tendaji smiled. "Then chill it is. Thank you, Raven. And for your kindness, I have a gift." Tendaji reached into his shoulder bag.

A gift? Raven thought. Ooh, this boy knows what I like!

Pulling out a white feather, Tendaji handed it to Raven. "Will you accept this feather?"

"A feather?" Raven repeated. Okaaay, maybe the boy *doesn't* know what I like. She was about to turn it down, but one look at Tendaji's face told her how excited he was to give it to her. Clearly, Tendaji thought this feather was a terrific gift. And maybe it was—in Shakobi. So Raven tried to sound enthusiastic. "It's a feather!" She took the white feather. "Sure. I've never really gotten a feather before." This, at least, was true.

Tendaji smiled, as if this was wonderful news. Like, maybe people gave Raven feathers every day. "I am very pleased to hear that." With a nod, he headed down the hall.

Eddie looked at the feather dubiously. "He gave you a feather, Rae?"

"Ooh," Chelsea teased, singsonging as though they were in the first grade, "Raven got a feather."

Raven shrugged. "Yeah, it's just a feather. It doesn't mean anything."

But down the hall, Tendaji was whispering into his cell phone. ". . . Yes . . ." he said. "Yes. She has accepted the sacred feather." He looked back at Raven, who still had the white feather in her hand.

Actually, the feather *did* mean something. Raven just didn't know it yet.

Later that afternoon, Raven, Chelsea, Eddie, and Tendaji were sitting at the coffee table doing their homework. So far, Raven really liked Tendaji. He had told them all about Shakobi, which sounded like a really interesting place. Tendaji had even been on a safari! And he was a sweet, thoughtful person. Even if he did think that a feather made a good present.

"Raven," Tendaji said, looking around, "thank you for inviting me to your lovely home."

Raven smiled. Lovely home, she thought. He thinks it's lovely—and I didn't even clean up!

"Yeah, now see, this is what we mean by chillin'," Eddie explained. He shoved a plate of sponge cakes topped with chocolate frosting across the coffee table. "Bingle Bong?" he offered.

Tendaji hesitated a moment, then chose one of the cakes. "It is golden. And spongy." He took a bite, and his eyes grew round. "And filled with a sweet, creamy-like substance. It is a miracle. What is in this?" He reached for the wrapper, but Raven snatched it away.

"Aww, nah homie," she said quickly, "you don't want to know."

Just then, Mrs. Baxter walked through the front door. She was loaded down with books. Raven's mom was studying law. And those lawyers know how to write some long books, Raven thought.

"Hey, kids," Mrs. Baxter said.

"Hey, Mom," Raven said, going over to her mother, "I want to introduce you to my friend Tendaji. He's an exchange student. Tendaji, meet my mother."

Tendaji looked startled. "You wish me to meet your mother?" He bowed deeply toward Mrs. Baxter and took her hand in his. "This is a great honor."

Mrs. Baxter giggled. "Well, that's very sweet of you, Tendaji," she said with a smile. "So, from where are you exchanging?"

"I am from the country of Shakobi."

"Shakobi," Mrs. Baxter repeated. "How interesting. I would love to hear all about your history, your customs, your natural resources—"

Oh, my gosh, Mom wants the whole oral report, Raven thought, rolling her eyes. "Okay, Mama," she said, shoving Mrs. Baxter toward the stairs. "Mama? Buh-bye."

Tendaji reached into his bag. "Now that I have met the mother of Raven," he said, handing Raven a seashell, "would you accept this shell?"

Oh, boy, Raven thought, here we go with the weird gifts. But she didn't want to be rude. "Uh-huh," she squeaked. "Uh, yeah. I'll accept this shell. I can put it next to my feather."

"As you should," Tendaji said seriously. "Now I must leave. This day has been as miraculous as a . . ." He searched for the perfect simile. ". . . cream-filled Bingle Bong."

Tendaji left, taking a bite of the Bingle Bong as he walked through the door.

Raven looked over at her best friends, who were grinning crazily.

"Ooh," Chelsea teased, poking Raven in the shoulder. "Raven got a shell. Wow, Rae, I think he likes you."

Raven gave her friend a heavy-lidded look. "Chels, it's a feather and a shell. I mean how serious could it be?" With a sigh, she got back to studying.

Good question.

Because right outside the front door, Tendaji was on his cell phone again. "It has become serious," he said into the receiver. "She has introduced me to her mother. So I offered her the seashell . . ." He smiled. "Yes, Father, I know the next step."

He closed his cell phone and walked off. This was quickly turning into the best day of Tendaji's life.

Chapter Two

Cory's pet rat, Lionel, leaned in for a closer look at the computer screen. Lionel was perched on Cory's shoulder as Cory typed away at the keyboard. "Okay, Lionel," Cory said, "before we check out the contest results, I want you to remember that winning isn't everything." He gave his rat a serious look, then pressed ENTER.

"We won!" Cory shouted. "We won! We won! We won!" He pulled his black-and-white pet off his shoulder and looked into his beady eyes. "I lied, Lionel," Cory admitted. "Winning *is* everything! We won!"

Hearing his son's shouts, Mr. Baxter walked into Cory's room carrying an armload of clean laundry. "We won?" he asked peering at the monitor. "What did we win?"

"Actually, Lionel won," Cory explained. "I sent in his picture to 'rate-my-pet-rat dot com' and he was voted 'most photogenic rat.'"

Mr. Baxter frowned at the onscreen image of Lionel. WINNER flashed beside the photo in huge, red letters. "Are you serious? What's the prize? A little ball of cheese?" Cory's dad cracked up at his own joke.

Cory rolled his eyes. "No," he said, as though that was the dumbest thing he had ever heard. "A *big* ball of cheese. And his picture's gonna be on the cover of *Rat Style* magazine."

"They got a magazine about rats?" Mr. Baxter laughed. "What do you do, read it or line his cage with it?" He opened Cory's drawer and plunked a pile of clean clothes inside.

Cory sighed. "Laugh now, Dad," he said. "But one day, when Lionel's famous, he's gonna have the last laugh."

Mr. Baxter looked at Lionel. His little whiskers twitched, as though he really *was* about to have the last laugh.

At the sound of the doorbell, Raven hurried down the stairs and flung open the door.

"Delivery for Raven Baxter," Eddie said brightly, holding out an enormous gift-wrapped box. Chelsea was standing right behind him, grinning.

Ooh, what could it be? Raven wondered. It isn't even my birthday! But I'm ready to accept presents any time! Eddie handed over the box but kept his hand held out. Raven gave his open palm a dubious glance. I hope he's not expecting a tip, she thought. Because my tip will be: forget it.

Raven slapped Eddie's palm. "My brother," she told him.

Giving up, Eddie put his palm down and followed Chelsea into the Baxters' living room.

"It's from Tendaji," Chelsea explained as Raven placed the huge box on the coffee table. "He said it's a Shakobian custom that this gift be delivered to you by your closest friends."

Raven eyed the pretty box. "Oooh, I hope it's not a box of feathers," she said. Her fingers hesitated over the enormous red and gold bow. "It's wrapped so beautifully. I hate to, you know, mess it up." Reaching down, she ripped off the bow, tore open the box and shoved aside the fluffy purple tissue paper. Inside was a red silk dress embroidered with gold thread. Raven's heart thumped as she held it up. "Now this is the kind of gift I'm talkin' about." She nodded with approval. Finally, Tendaji was getting the hang of this gift-giving thing. And he was clearly someone who understood that Raven had serious style.

"Ooh," Chelsea teased, poking Raven in the shoulder, "Raven got a dress."

Even Eddie seemed impressed. "And look at the bling-bling," he said, holding the dress up in front of himself. "If I was ever gonna wear a dress—"

Raven gave him a raised-eyebrow look. The mental image was just too vivid.

Apparently, it had popped into Eddie's mind, too. "I'm not gonna even finish that sentence," he decided, handing the dress back to Raven. He flapped his hands at the red gown. "Just go on, take the dress away."

Just then, Mrs. Baxter walked into the living room with a basket of clean towels.

"Mom, look at this fabulous gift Tendaji sent me!" Raven held up the silk dress.

"Oh, it's gorgeous," Mrs. Baxter gushed,

walking over to get a closer look. She looked up at her daughter. "Give it back."

Raven's jaw dropped. "What?" she cried. "Why? Mom?"

"Honey," Mrs. Baxter said in a patient voice, "you cannot accept this dress. It's way too extravagant."

Oh, that is so like my mom! Raven thought furiously. Tendaji finally gives me something nice, and I can't even keep it!

"Yeah, Rae," Chelsea agreed, "it's way better than the feather and shell he got you."

Mrs. Baxter's eyebrows shot halfway up her forehead. "He gave you other gifts?"

"Well, Mom, kinda," Raven hedged. "I wouldn't call them gifts. More like . . . stuff you could, you know, find on the beach."

Raven's mother looked at the gorgeous embroidered dress. "Well, he didn't find this outfit on the beach," she pointed out. "He's obviously very serious about you. If you accept it, you'll be sending him the wrong message."

Wrong message? Raven thought. "Well, what about if I give him back the feather and the shell, and I keep the dress?" she suggested.

Mrs. Baxter sighed. "Raven . . ."

"Yeah . . ." She doesn't need to say it. I know what's coming.

"Pack up the dress and take it back," Mrs. Baxter ordered.

Raven looked at the dress, whimpering, as her mother stalked out of the room. I knew it was coming, but it still hurts to hear it out loud, she thought.

Chapter Three

Cory and Mr. Baxter stood back to watch as Lionel posed on a western set. He was dressed in a bandanna and a black hat—cowboy style. *Rat Style* magazine, had sent over a photographer named Aldo. Cory couldn't help admiring how comfortable Lionel seemed in front of the camera as Aldo snapped away.

Mr. Baxter, meanwhile, couldn't help thinking that Aldo was taking his own rat style way too seriously. The photographer had on an all-black outfit, over which he wore a gray fake-fur vest. He wore a beret, and his front teeth stuck out in an eerily similar way to Lionel's.

"Give me some good . . ." Aldo told Lionel as his flashbulb popped. "Give me some bad . . ." He snapped another shot. "Give me some ugly."

"How can you tell the difference?" Mr. Baxter muttered, laughing to himself.

Aldo tsk-tsked. "Who said that?" he demanded, his rodent teeth snapping as he wheeled to face Mr. Baxter and popped a flashbulb in his face. "Was that you?" Throwing up his hands, Aldo turned to Cory. "I can't work with this man in the room."

"Dad, don't laugh in front of Aldo," Cory said. "He is the top rodent photographer in the world."

"Ooh, say no more." Mr. Baxter nodded seriously. "If you need me, I'll be laughing in the hall." Snickering, he walked out of Cory's room.

"Sorry, Aldo," Cory apologized. "I guess my dad thinks this is all silly."

"Silly?" Aldo hissed. "I've been photographing

rats for twenty years and believe me, Lionel has the whole package!" He pursed his lips. "Silky whiskers, beady eyes, and a tail that just won't quit."

Cory nodded. "I've always known that."

"Trust me," Aldo said, holding up his camera, "Lionel's gonna be huge. Remember son," he gestured grandly, "'rats' spelled backward is 'star.'"

Cory gazed off into the distance. He could see it now—Lionel's name in lights.

There was no question about it—this rat was going somewhere.

Eddie and Chelsea watched as Raven snuffled, then packed the gorgeous gown back into its box. "Good-bye," she choked, "my beautiful dress."

Eddie patted her on the shoulder. "You're doing the right thing, Rae."

Raven swallowed hard. "I know."

"Yeah, Rae," Chelsea chimed in, "it doesn't matter that it's the most beautiful, gorgeous, breathtaking dress you'll ever wear in your entire life."

Raven glared at her best girlfriend. "Do you want me to pack you in this box, as well?"

Through her eye
The vision runs
Flash of future
Here it comes—

Whoa. Where am I? This place is gorgeous! All those people in beautiful African fabrics. . . . Oh, I need to find out where they are getting the goods. I could make some sweet outfits with that purple silk stuff over there.

And the beat. It's bumpin'! I dig this tribal music.

Oh, hey—oh, my. That's a group of good-looking dancers right there.

It's almost like I've landed in . . . Shakobi.

And speaking of Shakobi—is that Tendaji on that litter over there? Hello, nice to get carried around on a thronelike thing. It's almost like he's . . .

"All hail Prince Tendaji!"

Prince Tendaji? Oh, snap! I knew he was charming, but I didn't know he was Prince Charming!

"All hail Prince Tendaji."

Yeah, all hail! I'm hanging with a prince! And Eddie even fed him a Bingle Bong!

"Oh, my goodness!" Raven said as she snapped back into the present. She turned to Chelsea and Eddie. "You are never going to believe what I just saw. Tendaji? He's a prince."

Eddie looked stunned. "For real?"

"For reals," Raven squealed. "For reals."

"Wait a minute," Chelsea said, "if he's a prince, then you're like, you know, Cinderella. I mean, come on, all you need is for someone to come up to your door and ask you to the ball."

Ding-dong!

Raven looked at the door. That was some fast service. "Wow," she said, exchanging a look with Chelsea. Why doesn't my girl ever suggest having someone from the Publishers Clearing House come over to let me know about my prize winnings?

Raven hurried over to the door and flung it open. A messenger dressed in a bright tunic over loose pants stood there offering a scroll on a velvet pillow. He bowed to Raven and handed her the parchment. "From Prince Tendaji," he said in an official voice.

With a scream, Raven grabbed the scroll

and slammed the door in the messenger's face. She unrolled the handmade paper and the calligraphy. "It's an invitation," she announced. "He's throwing a party at the embassy!"

"Oh, my gosh," Chelsea cried. "It really *is* a ball!"

Suddenly, Raven's vision made sense. A party with people in Shakobian garb. African drumming. Tribal dancers. Tendaji on a litter . . . "Hey, hey, this must've been the party I saw in my vision!" Raven announced. "And let me tell you—the party? It was on."

"Yeah, that's gonna be so fun!" Chelsea agreed. She thought for a moment. "Wait a minute. Too bad you can't go."

Ooh, I hate it when my girl stops to think. It's never good. "Why can't I go?" Raven demanded.

Eddie looked at her from under heavy eyelids and gestured to the red silk gown.

"Because your mama said you've got to return that dress."

"Oh . . ." Raven cleared her throat. She knew one thing—she was going to that party. Think! she commanded herself. Think. Okay, there has to be a loophole. There's always a loophole! "Uh, I can return the dress . . . after I party with the prince."

Chelsea heaved a dreamy sigh. "Now, if only you had some glass slippers," she said.

I've got some gold sandals that will do just as well, Raven thought. And let's be honest . . . what Mama doesn't know won't hurt her a bit.

Chapter Four

Chelsea and Eddie were sitting in Raven's kitchen, nibbling on some of the snacks they had found in the fridge. Raven had just left for the ball, but Chelsea and Eddie had stayed behind. There was no point in going over to one of *their* houses. Everyone knew the Baxters had the best snacks. "I can't believe Raven lied to her mom about returning that dress," Chelsea said.

"Technically, she didn't lie," Eddie pointed out. "She is returning the dress. She's just gonna party in it first."

At that moment, Mrs. Baxter bounded down the back stairs and into the kitchen. "Where's Raven?" She was breathless. "Did she go to return that dress?"

Chelsea thought for a moment. "Well, technically . . ."

Eddie broke in. "What she means, Mrs. B, is, uh, Raven and the dress both left."

Mrs. Baxter heaved a sigh of relief. "That's good, because I did some research on the Internet." She shook her head. "It turns out, Tendaji is a prince."

Eddie and Chelsea gaped at each other, pretending to be shocked.

"Noooo," they chorused.

Mrs. Baxter nodded. "It's true," she told them. "And in his country, accepting a feather, a shell, and a dress is a promise to be married."

Eddie and Chelsea gaped at each other again. Only this time, they really *were* shocked.

"Noooo!" they said together.

Mrs. Baxter let out a little giggle. "If she accepted that dress, she'd be on her way to her wedding right now." Raven's mother left the room.

"Raven's gonna walk into her own wedding!"

"I know!" Chelsea pouted. "Some best friend. She didn't even ask me to be a bridesmaid!"

"Forget about that," Eddie commanded. "We've got to go save Rae!"

Eddie and Chelsea rushed through the door. They had to stop that wedding!

"Oh, Cory," Aldo said as he munched on a hunk of Swiss cheese, "big news!" His fingers tapped the keyboard, and he peered at Cory's computer monitor. He had sent off the digital photos of Lionel an hour earlier and was checking his e-mail for a response. "*Rat Style* magazine loved the pictures!" Aldo squeaked. "And get this, they want to sign Lionel to an exclusive contract." This was standard procedure for the magazine. Whenever they found a talented rat, they gave him a contract. They didn't want to lose talent like Lionel to *Rodent Life* or *Vermin Weekly*.

"You hear that, buddy?" Cory squealed to his best friend/famous pet rat. "You're gonna be a star!" He turned to Aldo, his voice serious. "Okay, now let's talk about the dough-re-me."

Aldo snickered. "Oh, there'll be plenty of that."

Cory folded his arms across his chest. "Could you be a little more specific?"

Pulling out a pad and pen, Aldo started to scribble. There were a lot of zeros involved. "The dollar amount of the offer will be roughly in this neighborhood." He handed the pad to Cory, whose eyes went wide at the figure.

"Ooh, I'd like to live in that neighborhood, baby!" Cory stuck out his hand. "You've got yourself a deal."

Cory and Aldo shook on it. Cory was sure that Lionel would have shaken hands, too, if he could.

After all, Lionel was the star. Cory was doing all of this for him.

The Shakobian ambassador smoothed his long purple tunic as he looked around the embassy. He couldn't help feeling nervous—it was his responsibility to make sure that everything was perfect for the prince's wedding. The king himself had telephoned to make sure that all was arranged according to custom. The ambassador had put his entire staff on the project. There were so many details—and he hadn't had much advance notice!

The ambassador called over two of the embassy's strongest bodyguards. "When our future princess arrives, as our tradition commands, her feet must never touch the ground," he reminded them. The bodyguards nodded. They knew the custom as well as the ambassador did.

Just then, Raven walked through the door wearing the gorgeous red dress.

And this dress isn't the only thing looking gorgeous, she thought, as she floated into the room. After all, it fit like a glove. The rich color brought out the brightness in Raven's eyes, and she had done her makeup and hair with special care. This was, after all, her first royal ball!

"Hey," Raven said, looking around the room, which was crowded with elegant guests, "it is on." African drum music thumped in the background.

Just then, two strong guys walked up to Raven.

That's what I'm talking about, Raven thought, looks like I've got it . . . whoa! Raven let out a little squeal as the guys lifted her off her feet. "Okay, going up," she said cheerfully. I guess this is some kind of Shakobian custom, she decided. They certainly know how to treat their guests!

Just roll with it, Raven decided. After all, these people thought a feather made a great gift. Who knew what other weird traditions they might have? "Okay, thank you," Raven said to the guys. "Y'all know how to greet a guest." The two men carried Raven toward a small platform. "Thank you, but I could've walked up. Okay, I guess we're going down," she said as the guys lowered her into an elaborately carved chair.

Geez, this chair is supersized, Raven thought. Her feet were dangling off the edge— nowhere near the floor. But there was one advantage to being so high up—she had a good view of the crowd. "Yeah, I like this seat a lot better," she told the guys. "Ya'll were right."

An attendant placed a jeweled crown on her head. "Ooh, I love accessories!" Raven gushed. "Let me hook you up, homie." But before she could get her man the hookup, another attendant appeared with a platter of fruit. He popped a purple grape into Raven's mouth.

Mmmm, that's some tasty fruit! This is definitely better than that Bingle Bong we gave Tendaji! "These are really good!" Raven said. She gestured for more grapes. "You can keep those coming. I like 'em."

The ambassador scurried over to introduce himself. "I am Dikembe," he said with a huge smile.

Raven gave him a little wave. "Hi."

"The Shakobian ambassador," Dikembe explained, bowing slightly.

"And I am Raven." Raven gestured for another grape.

"Yes, I know." Dikembe smiled. "We've been waiting for you." He turned and called, "Let the bell of welcome ring!" He clapped his hands, and a servant hurried over to pull a thick, braided cord that hung from the ceiling.

Instead of the loud gong that Raven was expecting, a soft tinkle chimed through the room.

Hmm, that's sort of the "jingle bell" of welcome, Raven thought, but she smiled politely.

The ambassador looked sheepish. "The actual bell has not yet arrived from Shakobi," Dikembe explained.

"It's okay," Raven assured him. "I still feel welcomed."

Dikembe beamed. "Excellent. Then let the dance begin!" An African dance troupe stormed into the party, performing their intricate moves. He turned to Raven. "Luckily, they *have* arrived from Shakobi." With another clap, the drumming swelled.

Oh, snap—these people are good! Raven thought as she bopped along in her seat to the music. I wish I could move like that! But I'd probably break something if I tried. She opened her mouth, and the attendant stuffed another grape inside. Now, I could get used to this lifestyle. "Mmmm," Raven said. "I'm liking this. Gimme those grapes."

Suddenly, two new dancers busted into the troupe. They were dressed like the others, but . . .

Those two dancers need a tutorial, Raven thought. They are seriously rhythm deprived. Hey—wait a minute. . . .

The two dancers bounced over to Raven.

Those aren't dancers, she realized. That's Eddie and Chelsea! "Psst . . . Rae," Chelsea whispered.

"What are you guys doing here?" Raven

demanded. She eyed their fake-fur outfits. "And why are you dressed like that? You ain't from Shakobi."

"Rae, we came down here to tell you that this is not a party," Eddie explained. "It's a wedding."

"Oh, a wedding?" Raven cried. She opened her mouth wide, and an attendant shoved in another grape. "I love weddings." She pressed her lips together. "I hope I don't cry."

"Oh, you gonna cry, all right," Eddie assured her. "Because it's your wedding, and you're gonna be the bride."

Raven nearly choked on her grape. "Raven gonna be what?"

"Look," Eddie said, cutting to the chase, "all of those gifts were Tendaji's way of proposing to you, all right?"

"See, Rae," Chelsea said in her first-grader voice, "I told you he liked you."

"Yes," Eddie went on, "and since you put on the dress and came down here, you accepted."

Raven's chin trembled. How am I going to get out of this? Suddenly, she felt like she was surrounded. Surrounded by people who wanted her to marry Tendaji!

Then again, Tendaji is a prince, Raven thought. If I married him, I'd probably get to sit around eating those grapes all long. . . .

Stop it! Stop it! she commanded herself. You have to focus on getting out of here. What if they don't let me go? Will I have to move to Shakobi? "Why didn't I listen to my mommy?" she wailed.

Dikembe stepped in front of Raven and clapped. At that moment, the drums and dancers stopped. "Presenting the new official currency of Shakobi . . . 'the Raven.'" He clapped again, and two attendants brought out an enormous reproduction of a five-dollar bill. Only it wasn't for five dollars—it was for five Ravens. And Raven's picture was right in the center!

The crowd cheered.

Dang, I look good with my face on that money, Raven thought. She waved to the crowd. It wasn't like she had much choice.

Cory smiled smugly as his parents studied the papers in front of them. Even they seemed amazed by the "neighborhood" Lionel's exclusive contract had put them in. "So, what do you think of that contract, Dad?"

"Looks like Lionel's gonna be makin' some serious cheddar," Mr. Baxter said. "I always knew that rat was gonna be a star."

"Dad, you were laughing at the whole thing," Cory corrected.

"Now I'm laughing all the way to the bank," Mr. Baxter shot back. He chuckled at his own joke.

"Thanks to Lionel, we can go on that Hawaiian vacation we always wanted," Cory said. An image of Lionel in a grass skirt floated through his mind.

"White sand," Mrs. Baxter said dreamily, "clear blue water, pineapple juice in a coconut cup. Mmmm, Mama like."

"Okay, son, sign right here." Mr. Baxter flipped to the last page of the contract and handed it to Cory, along with a pen.

The stairs creaked as Aldo appeared. He was carrying Lionel's cage—with Lionel inside. "Well, we're off to Paris," Aldo announced. He smiled, displaying his oversized front teeth. "Ooh-la-la!"

Cory frowned. "Uh, Paris?"

"Mm-hmm, it's the first stop on our

two-year world tour." Aldo held up the cage. "We'll send you a postcard."

"Au revoir, Lionel!" Mrs. Baxter called. Then, picturing the white sand beaches of Hawaii, she added, "Or should I say, 'aloha'?"

Aldo reached for the papers. "I'll just need that signed contract."

Cory looked down at the dotted line. . . .

But all he could see was Lionel's face.

He remembered all the times he had tucked Lionel into bed. He'd put a little nightcap on Lionel's head, so he wouldn't get cold, and read him his favorite book, *Good Night, Rat.* . . .

He remembered spending quality time with Lionel on his shoulder, hanging out and watching TV. . . .

He remembered playing with Lionel's see-saw. Corey would push one side, giving Lionel a ride up and down. . . .

So many good times. So many fond memories . . .

"Cory!" Mr. Baxter shook Cory's shoulder, snapping him back to reality.

"The deal's off," Cory announced, before he even had a chance to think about what he was saying.

"What?" Aldo cried.

"What?" Mr. Baxter cried.

"I'm sorry," Cory said as he grabbed his pet's cage, "but Lionel's my best friend."

Mr. Baxter looked doubtful. "I thought money was your best friend."

"Wow, Victor," Mrs. Baxter said, "sounds like Cory's made up his mind." She sighed. "No matter what Mama like."

Aldo narrowed his beady eyes and tsked through his teeth. "This is why I don't work with humans," he huffed. Then he breezed out the door.

Cory shrugged and looked down at his best friend, who was curled up in his cage, asleep. Cory knew that he would miss the money—and the trip to Hawaii—but he was glad that he didn't let his best friend go.

After all, how many people besides Cory realized that Lionel was more than just a pretty face?

Chapter Five

Two handsome attendants fanned Raven with enormous feather fans, and she was starting to think that becoming a princess wasn't so bad, after all.

No! Stop it, she told herself. You are not going to become a princess. You won't have your name on a five-Raven bill. You won't wear gorgeous silk clothes and get fanned by hotties. You won't eat grapes at every meal. You will stay in San Francisco with your parents. And Cory.

Raven whimpered. Okay, I have to do this—now, she decided. "Where in the world's Tendaji?" she asked.

"Look, I don't know, Rae." Eddie craned his

neck to look around the room. "But you can't wait any longer. We've got to get out of here, girl!"

"Okay!" Right. Gotta get out of here—while I'm still single. "You go see if the coast is clear."

Eddie hustled off.

"And Chels, you check the other exit over there," she told her best girlfriend. Chelsea didn't ask questions—she just leaped into action.

Raven moved forward to get off the throne, but she was too slow. Two attendants rushed over and swept her off her feet. "You guys, it's okay," Raven told them. "I can walk." But the attendants weren't having it. They put Raven on a ceremonial litter held aloft by four muscular men. "Aw, okay," Raven said, surrendering, "I can ride on the little tray. It's cool." Looks like sneaking out of here is going to be a little more challenging than I thought, Raven decided as the strongmen lifted her litter onto their shoulders. "Up we go!" Raven chirped, trying to seem cheerful. "I guess . . ."

Ambassador Dikembe gestured for the crowd's attention. "All hail Prince Tendaji!" he called.

The drums beat in earnest and the dancers broke into joyful movement as Tendaji entered the embassy—on a ceremonial litter. He waved proudly.

"All hail Prince Tendaji," the crowd chanted, bowing to the prince.

"Just like my vision," Raven muttered. Only I didn't see the part where I was getting hauled around on a giant stretcher, too!

"And all hail our next princess," Dikembe announced. "Princess Raven!"

Princess Raven? You have to admit, that does sound good.

"All hail Princess Raven!" The crowd let out a wild cheer, snapping Raven back to reality.

"Nah. No." Raven flapped her hands. "No hailin'. Shhhh, people, shhhh. Not necessary. Shhhh."

Tendaji's attendants steered his litter so that he came to a stop beside Raven. He gave her a vibrant smile. "My princess," he said warmly.

Ouch, Raven thought. Tendaji is so sweet. How am I going to let him down easy—without embarrassing him in front of all of these people? "Uh, yeah, Tendaji, we got to talk about this 'princess situation' . . ." Raven started.

"Yes!" Tendaji agreed. "But first, we dance!"

Dance? Oh, that sounds—

"What?" Raven cried as her seat began to buck and roll like a small boat in a perfect storm. Raven's attendants had begun bouncing her litter to the beat of the Shakobian drums. She grabbed the sides in an effort not to fall off as Tendaji's litter bounced away. *Oh, no! I have to talk to him, before we bounce into matrimony!* "Oh, okay," Raven said, trying to just go with her new litter-seat "dancing." "Oh, okay. No. Follow the prince." She pointed, so that the attendants would understand what she was saying. "You know what a prince is."

The attendants tried to obey. They bounced toward Tendaji. But they were bouncing so fiercely that Raven nearly fell off!

Oooh, those grapes are about to make a reappearance, Raven thought as her litter rocked back and forth. "Okay, speed bump happening," Raven announced. Her tiara started to fall off. "Losin' my crown though, people. Oh, okay. I'm not really dancing like I should be. So, maybe we should slow it down a little bit and get this right."

Ambassador Dikembe stepped through the crowd. "Attention, everyone!" he shouted. "To the marriage altar." He gave a quick double clap.

"To the marriage altar!" he repeated.

Raven's litter rocked again as her attendants started toward the altar. Okay, Raven decided, this has been fun, but the madness has to end. "No, fellas, this is my stop," she announced, grabbing the rope to the Bell of Welcome. With a fierce yank, she pulled herself off the litter. . . .

Whoa!

"Okay, I'll stop!" Raven shouted. There was a cheerful jingling as Raven swung through the air. Back and forth over the crowd.

Wow—way to make a subtle exit! she thought madly as she flew past the stunned ambassador.

"Stop!" she cried.

The crowd gasped as Raven went on with her Tarzan imitation. A few of the attendants chased her to keep her from falling, but Raven lost her grip.

Chelsea and Eddie gaped as Raven landed smack on the ceremonial litter—right back where she started. "Nice catch, fellas," Raven told the attendants.

"My princess-to-be," Tendaji cried as his attendants carried him toward Raven, "are you okay?"

Raven sighed. This wasn't going to be easy. "Tendaji, man, we gotta talk."

"We will have plenty of time for that after the wedding," Tendaji assured her.

"No," Raven shook her head. "There's not gonna be a wedding."

"What?" Tendaji cried. "Why not?"

"No, you don't understand," Raven told him. Her voice softened. "I think you're great.

You're nice, you're sweet, and dude, you're like a, you're like a total prince."

Tendaji had to agree. "It's true. I am a total prince."

"But I'm too young," Raven explained. "If I had known what all those gifts meant, I never would've led you on." She winced. "I'm sorry."

Tendaji nodded, as though he understood completely. "It is I who should apologize to you," he said. "In my country, we believe in marriage at first sight."

"Oh." Well, that's a new one, Raven thought. Marriage at first sight? Well, at least nobody has to suffer through a first date. "I guess our customs are pretty different," she said. Raven peered around the room at all the confused guests. She knew she was really letting Tendaji down. "Look, I'm sorry I ruined our wedding. I hope you'll forgive me."

Wincing, she gave him a hopeful look. "Can we still be friends?" Raven asked.

"Of course," Tendaji said warmly. "And even if we are not married, you will always be my princess." He leaned toward Raven and wrapped her in a huge hug.

Raven sighed. Tendaji really was a great guy. He was going to make some princess really happy someday.

But not today.

"All right, boys," Raven said to her attendants, "you can let me down now."

Tendaji snapped his fingers. The attendants lowered the litter and Raven stepped off.

"Raven!" the ambassador cried, running over. "Your feet have touched the ground."

"What?" Raven cried, looking at the floor. "Why? Is something wrong with the ground?"

"Only in the sense that you have disgraced our entire country," Dikembe replied. "So to remove our shame, we must ceremoniously shave your head."

Raven touched her head. My gorgeous hair! No, no! Cut off my leg—don't take my hair! "Please, please, please," she begged, "don't shave my head! Please."

Tendaji's attendants had lowered him to the floor, too, and he and the ambassador exchanged a meaningful look.

"Okay," the ambassador said, breaking into a grin. "I'm only joking. The wedding is off, but the party is on!" He shrugged. "I didn't have the bell, anyway." He turned to the crowd. "Everybody, dance!"

Raven turned to Tendaji. That was a good one, she thought. These Shakobians have a good sense of humor. The drummers started up a bumpin' beat. "See," Raven said to Tendaji, "now that my feet are on the ground, I can show you how Americans get down. Hook it up, hook it up."

Raven led Tendaji to the dance floor, where Eddie and Chelsea were already grooving with the rest of the dance troupe. Raven busted out a few moves, and Tendaji did his best to keep up.

Dang, Raven thought as she moved to the beat, I would have made a good princess.

Oh, well. I guess I can still be a princess . . . in my own way.

"Yeah, Chels," Raven said into the phone a few hours later, "after I got back from the party I was so grounded. My parents were *so* mad about me sneaking out and almost getting married."

Actually, the Baxters had taken the news pretty well. They'd only yelled for forty-five minutes. Raven had been expecting at least two hours.

"Anyway," Raven went on, "I had to return all of Tendaji's gifts, including the wedding dress. But there is one gift I'm going to keep for a while."

Chelsea didn't even ask what it was. She already knew—of course, Raven wasn't keeping the shell or the feather. She was keeping the best gift.

"Anyway, I gotta go," Raven said. "I'm getting hungry. Okay, girl, I'll talk to you later."

Raven clicked off. It sure felt good to have friends like Chelsea and Eddie in her life. Without them, she'd be off to Shakobi right now!

And it was lucky that the Baxters had given in and let Raven keep this one little gift for a while. After what I've been through, Raven decided, I deserve something special! "Fellas," Raven said, gesturing to the four muscle-bound guys holding her litter, "kitchen."

The attendants hauled the litter onto their shoulders and headed toward the kitchen door.

Raven sighed happily. "I could get used to this."

Now if only I could get them to take next week's finals for me. . . .

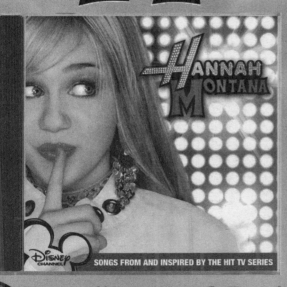

Face-off
From the hit TV series on Disney Channel

Keeping Secrets
With 8 pages of photos from the show!
From the hit TV series on Disney Channel

MUSIC'S BIGGEST STAR IS HER SCHOOL'S BIGGEST SECRET.

Truth or Dare
With 8 pages of photos from the show!
From the hit TV series on Disney Channel

COLLECT THEM ALL!

Super Sneak
With 8 pages of photos from the show!
From the hit TV series on Disney Channel

CHECK OUT THE NEW BOOK SERIES BASED ON THE HIT DISNEY CHANNEL SHOW!

Disney CHANNEL   **Disney** PRESS